SUPER SNAIL

ELYS DOLAN

Kevin was just a normal slug.

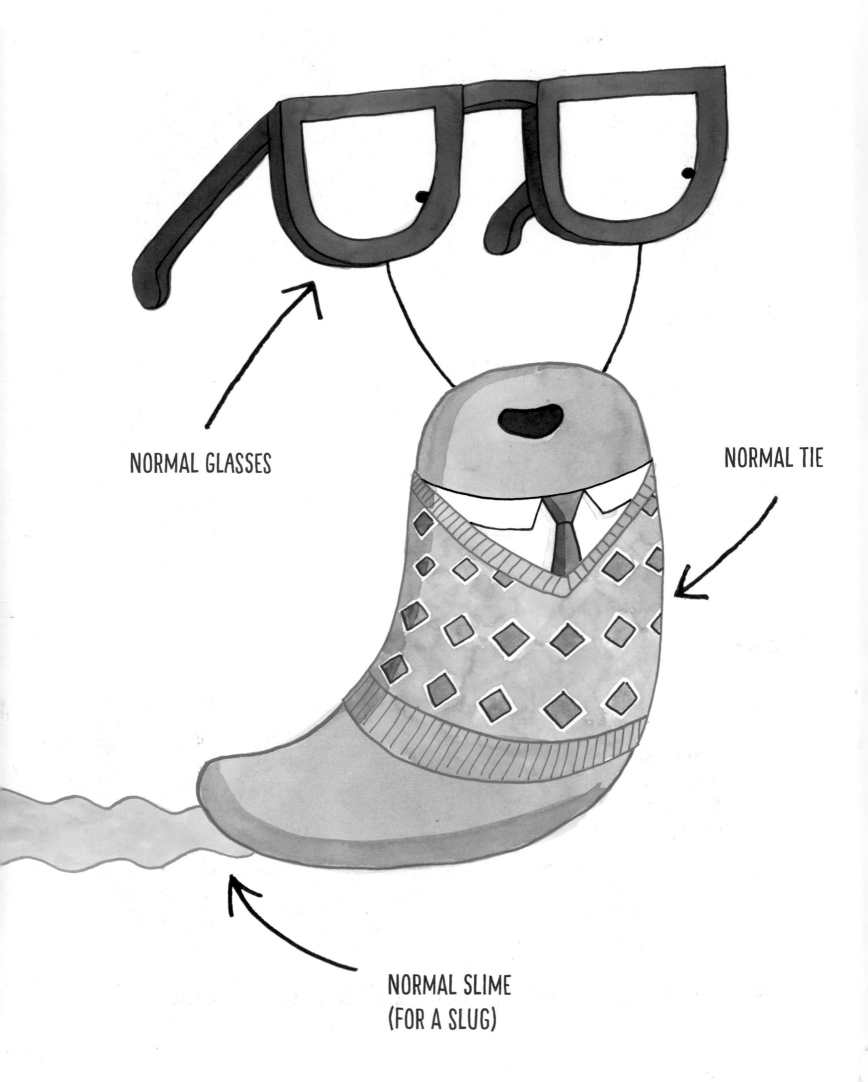

NORMAL GLASSES

NORMAL TIE

NORMAL SLIME
(FOR A SLUG)

He had a boring job.

A mean boss.

And he never got the girl.

But by night, Kevin put on his shell and became . . .

He was **FEARLESS.**

He was **INVINCIBLE.**

He was . . . **SLIMY!**

And that wasn't all.

Kevin had the best gadgets.

ROCKET BOOMERANG

NO ONE TOLD ME IT COMES BACK!

SMOKE SCREEN

COUGH COUGH!

BOUNCING BIKE

WEEE!

BOINK!

INVISIBILITY CLOAK

THIS WORKS REALLY WELL.

WAAHHH!

BANG

FIREWORK JET-SKI

LASER-SHOW PARACHUTE

WOW, SO MANY PRETTY COLOURS.

CORDLESS VACUUM

DUM-DE-DUM.

VAROOOM

He even thought he could fly if he tried hard enough.

Despite all this, Kevin still didn't feel like a real hero. He needed some advice.

Kevin went to see the League of Heroes because they were very brave, famous and good-looking. The League said he could prove himself by doing one of these things:

But it didn't quite go to plan . . .

Never fear though! A disaster was in progress downtown, so Kevin went to help.

However much he tried though,
he wasn't much help.

But it didn't seem to have the right effect on the villains.

Kevin had never felt less like a hero. He began to head home.

But when a report came over the radio, he realised there was one last thing he could try . . .

Reports suggest that a **SUPER VILLAIN** is attacking the city. Oh no! He's kidnapped a citizen . . .

OH, SOMEONE HELP!

SHOULD SIR GET A MOVE ON?

OH NO! THAT SOUNDS LIKE SUSAN, MY ONE TRUE LOVE! I HAVE TO HELP!

BEEP!

Kevin would have to find a way to take down Laser Pigeon.

Luckily Kevin had an idea.

NOT NOW, WILFRED. I'M TRYING TO FLY.

I'M SURE I'VE NEARLY GOT IT.

WAHHH!

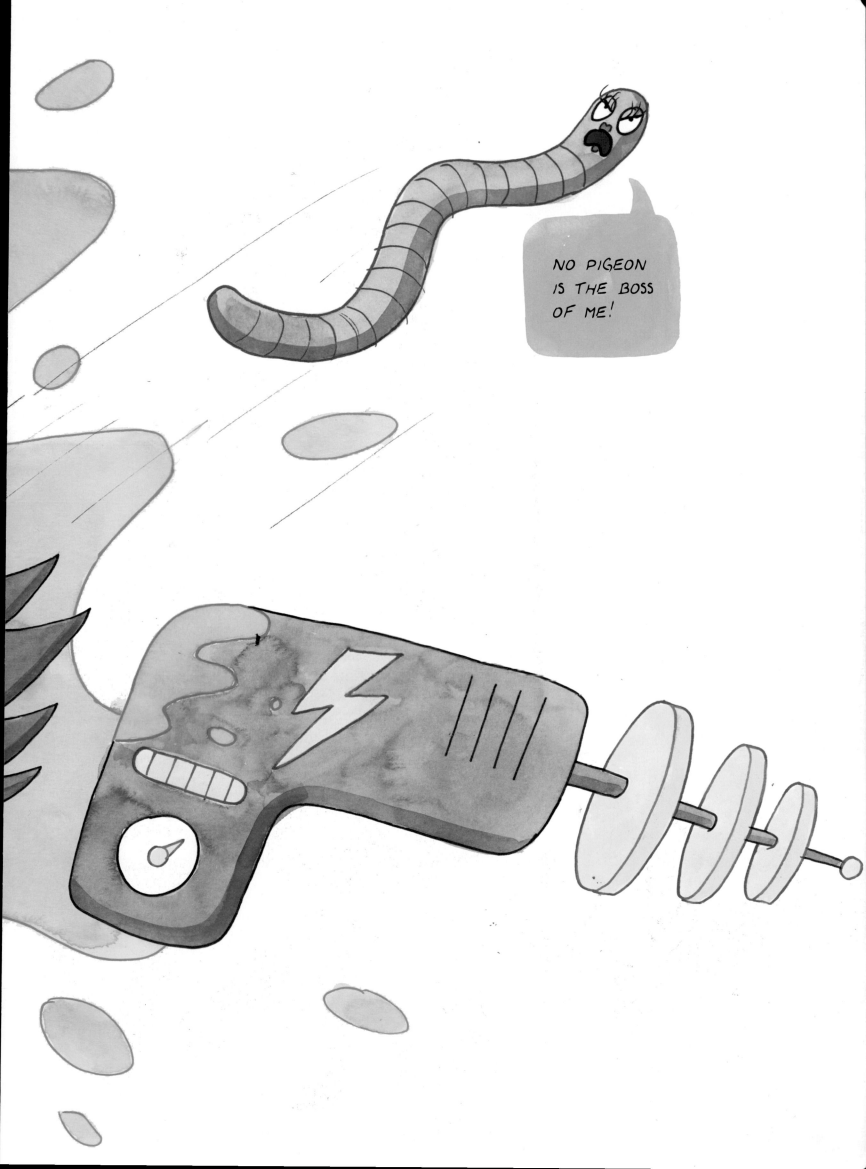

Laser Pigeon was defeated and the League of Heroes was terribly impressed by Super Snail.

Now Super Snail was officially a member of the League of Heroes and he had the most awesome of super powers . . .

PAY ATTENTION, SNAIL! WE CAN'T LET THOSE NINJA GUINEA PIGS GET AWAY!

PRIZE WINNING NOVEL

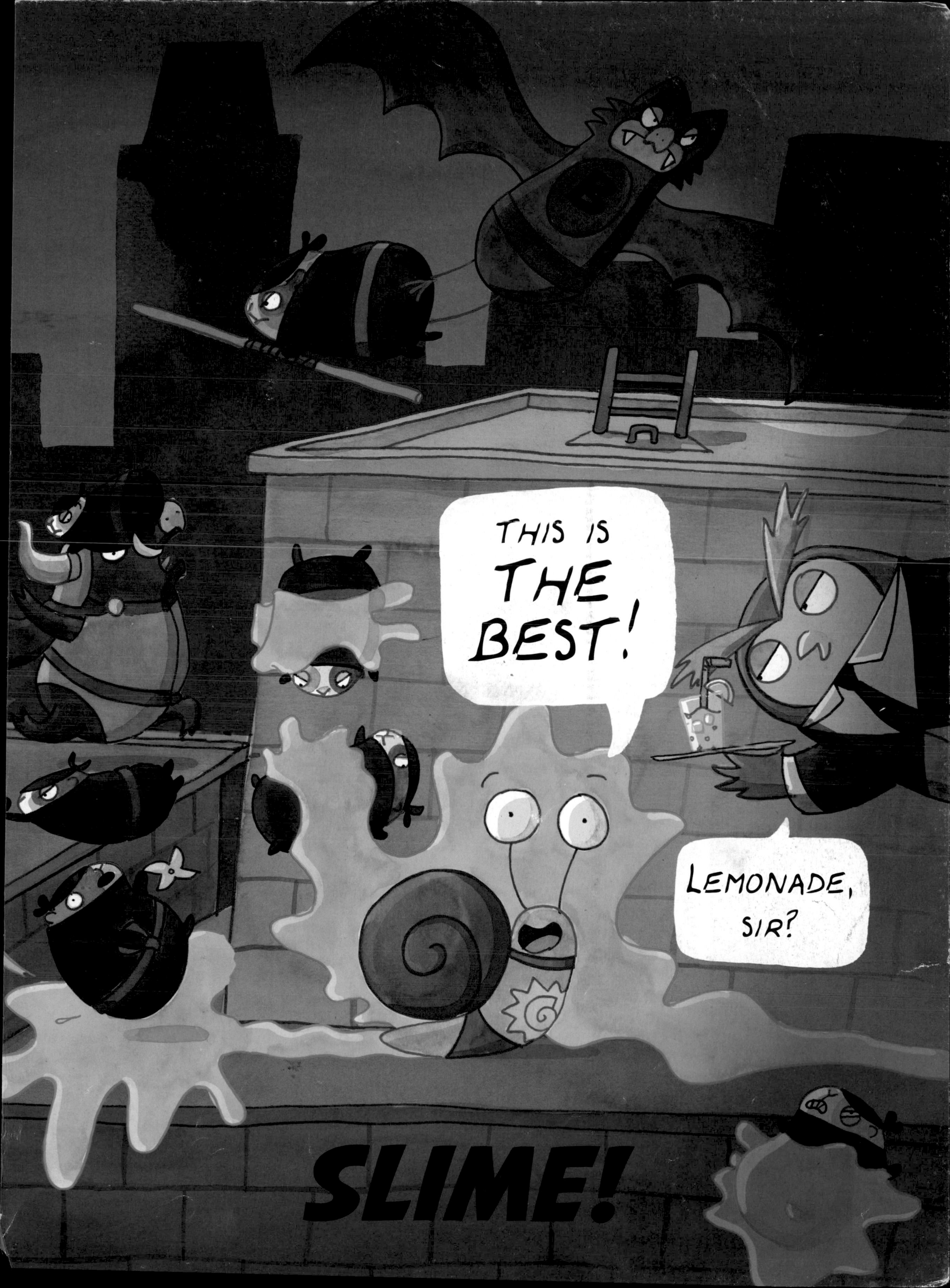
THIS IS THE BEST!
LEMONADE, SIR?
SLIME!

WELL THAT
WAS A GOOD
DAY'S WORK,
I THINK.

HODDER CHILDREN'S BOOKS

First published in Great Britain in 2019
by Hodder and Stoughton

Text and illustrations copyright © Elys Dolan, 2019

The right of Elys Dolan to be identified as the author and illustrator of this Work has been asserted by her in accordance
with the Copyright, Designs and Patents Act 1988.

A CIP catalogue record for this book is available from the British Library.

HB ISBN: 978 1 444 94039 8
PB ISBN: 978 1 444 94040 4

1 3 5 7 9 10 8 6 4 2

Printed and bound in China.

Hodder Children's Books
An imprint of Hachette Children's Group
Part of Hodder and Stoughton

Carmelite House, 50 Victoria Embankment, London, EC4Y 0DZ

An Hachette UK Company

www.hachette.co.uk
www.hachettechildrens.co.uk